carousel
Donald Crews

Greenwillow Books/New York

Library of Congress
Cataloging in Publication Data

Crews, Donald. Carousel.

Summary:
Brief text and illustrations
recreate a ride on a merry-go-round.
[1. Merry-go-round—Fiction] I. Title.
PZ7.C8682Car   [E]   82-3062
ISBN 0-688-00908-5
ISBN 0-688-00909-3 (lib. bdg.)   AACR2

Three paintings of the carousel—
the empty carousel, the calliope,
and the carousel with children—
were prepared as full-color collages.
The carousel with children was
then photographed, and the camera
was moved to simulate motion.
For the sound pages, three pieces
of full-color art were prepared
and similarly photographed.
The camera was a Nikon F
with a 105mm lens. The film
was 35mm Kodachrome Type A.

Copyright © 1982
by Donald Crews

Printed in the
United States of America
First Edition
10 9 8 7 6 5 4 3 2 1

FOR MAMANNINAMY

Still, empty.

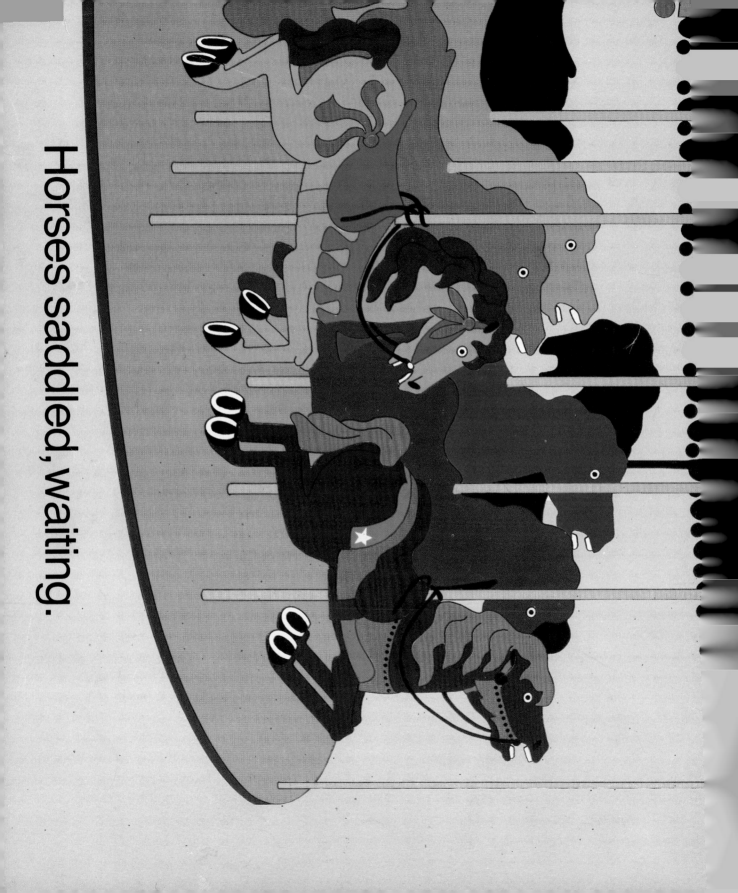

Horses saddled, waiting.

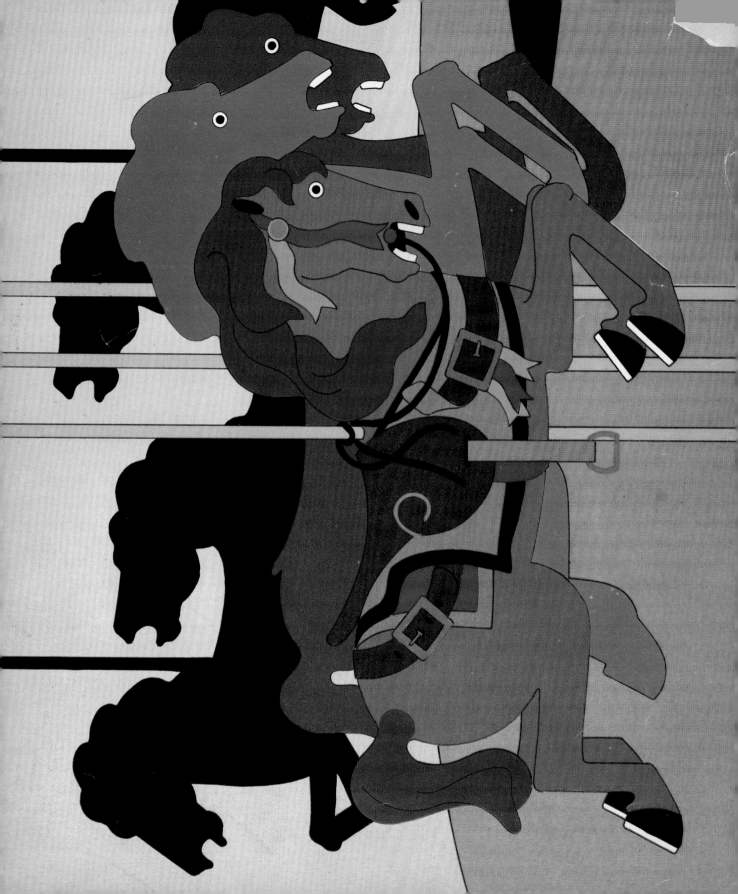

Calliope ready.

Riders up.

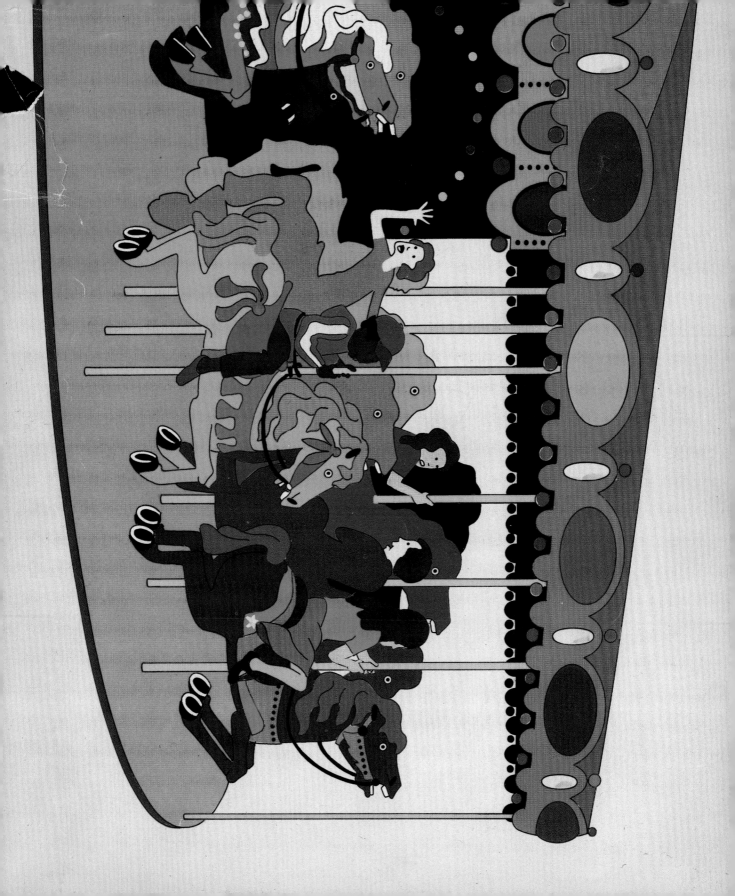

Music playing.

Horses off.

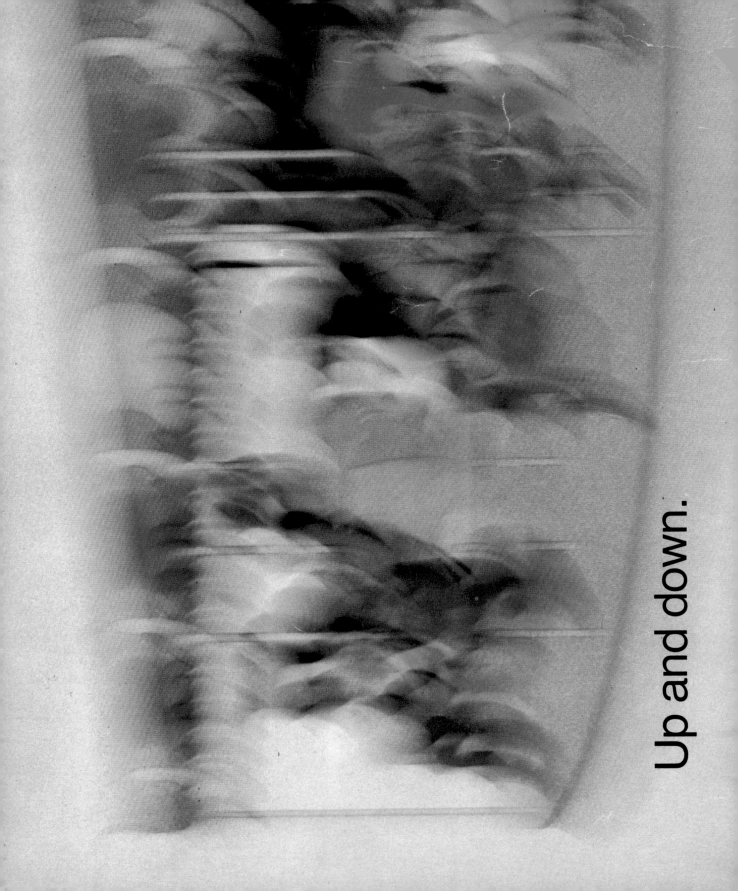

Up and down.

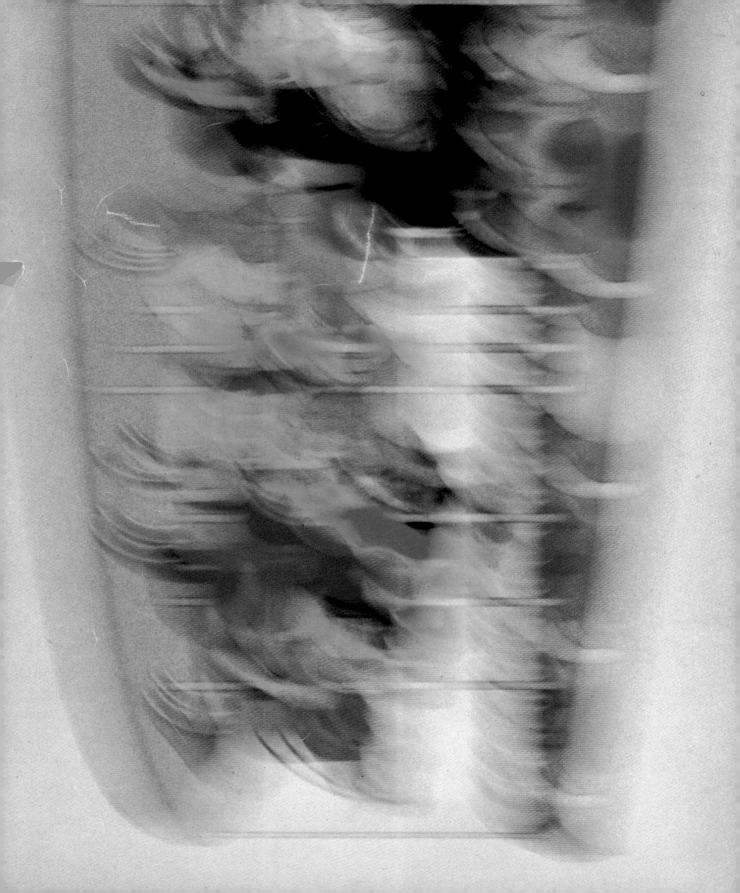

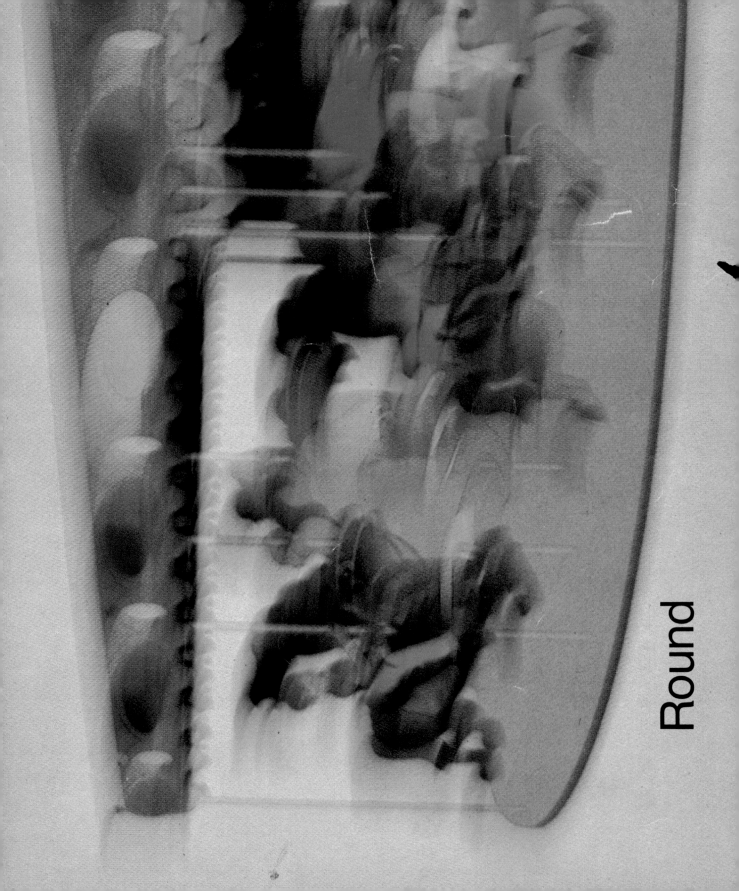

Round

and round.

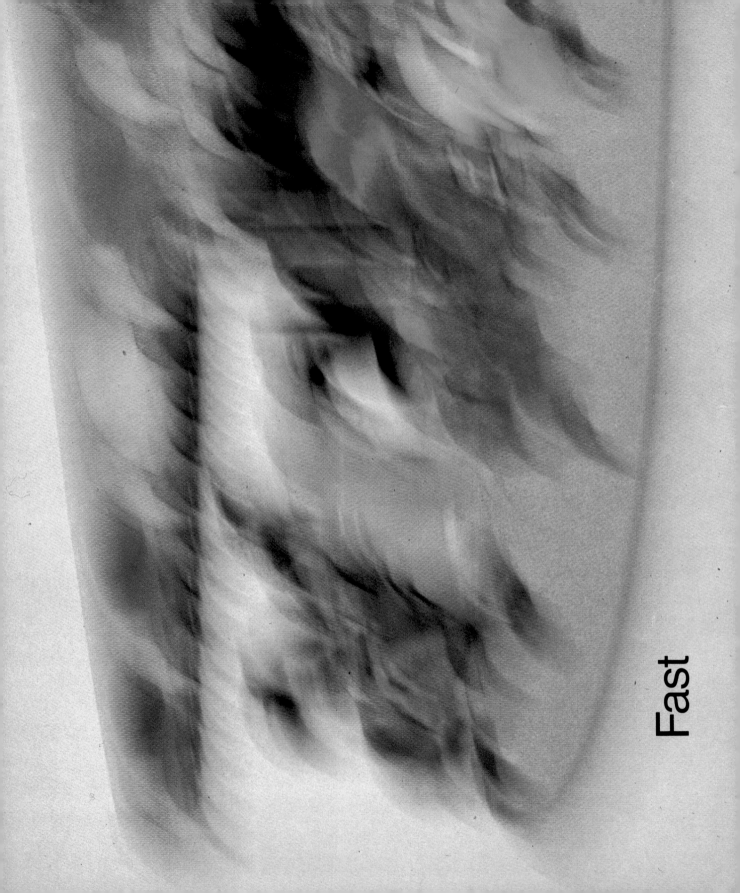

Fast

and faster.

Music blaring.

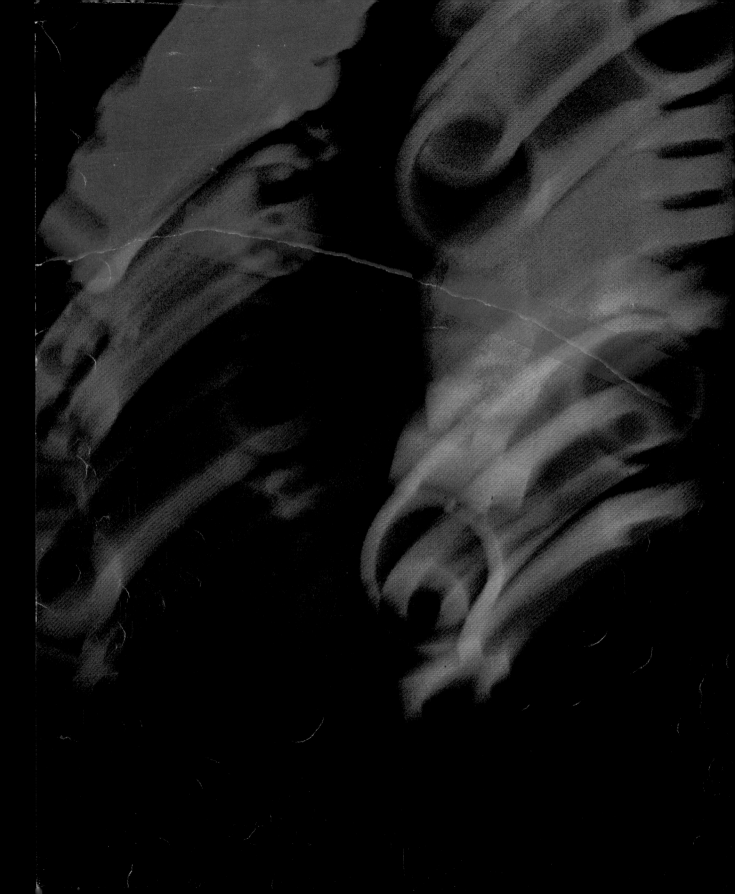

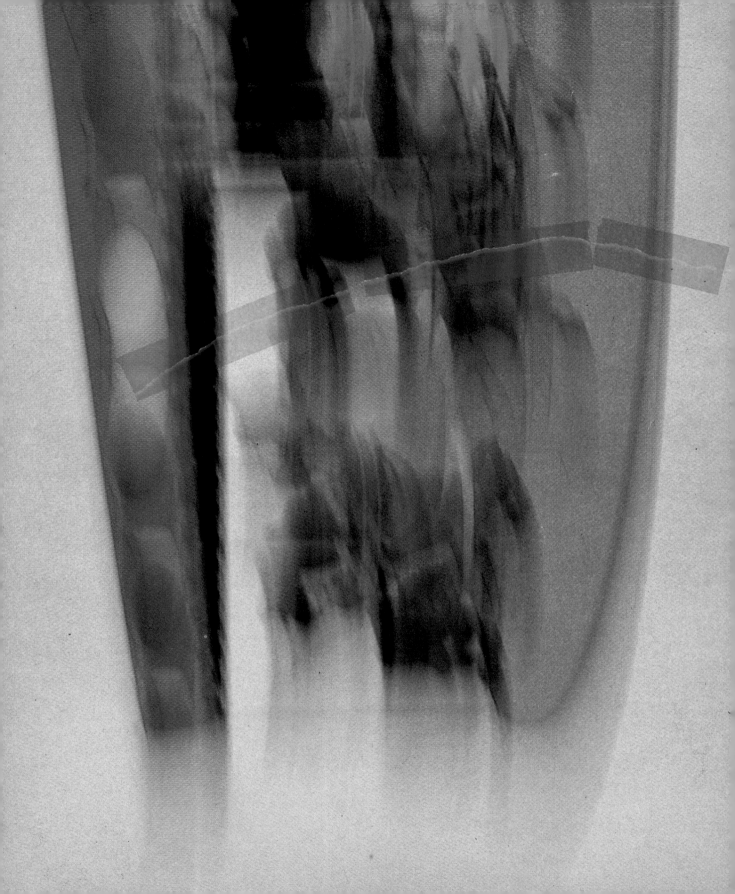

Horses racing.

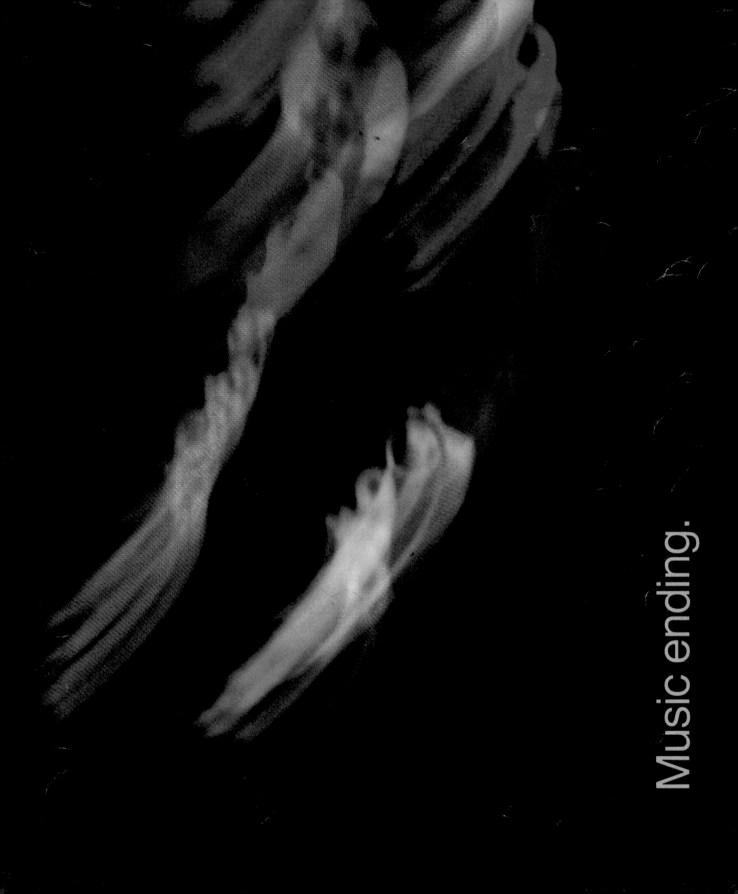

Music ending.

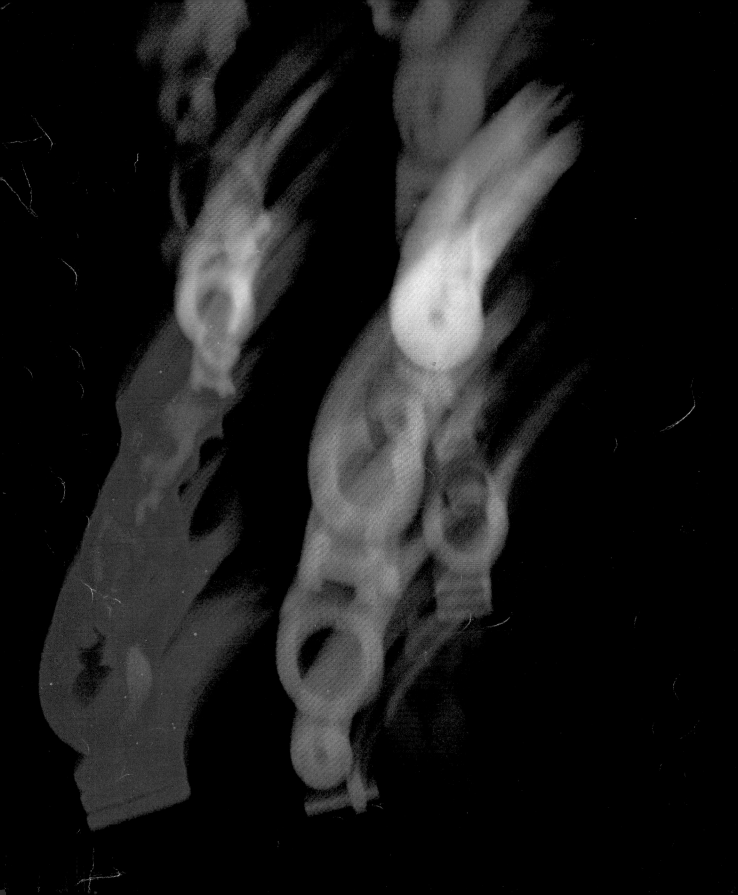

Horses slowing.

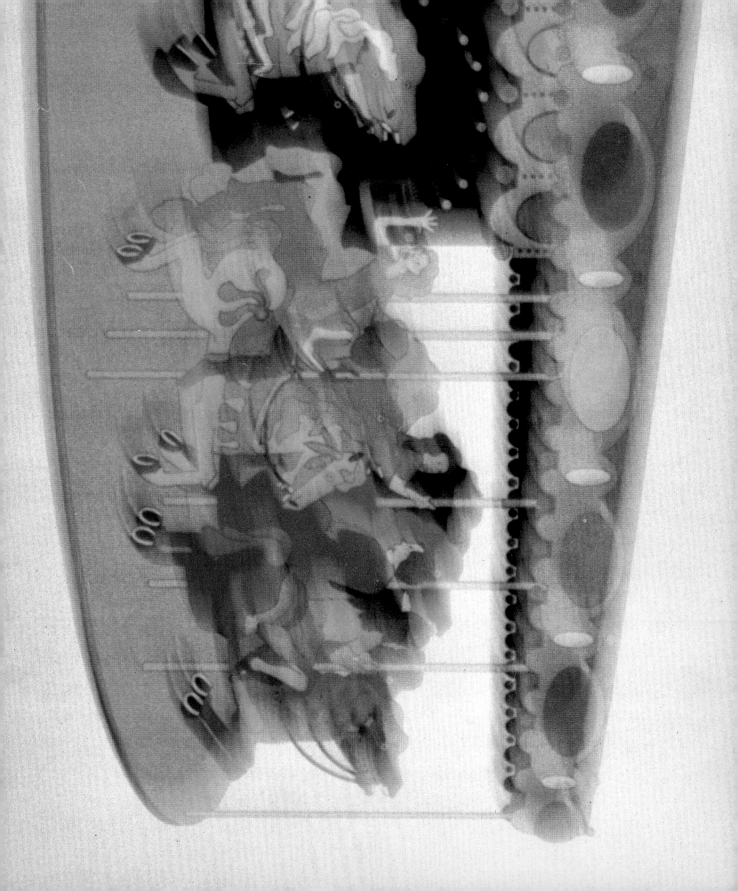

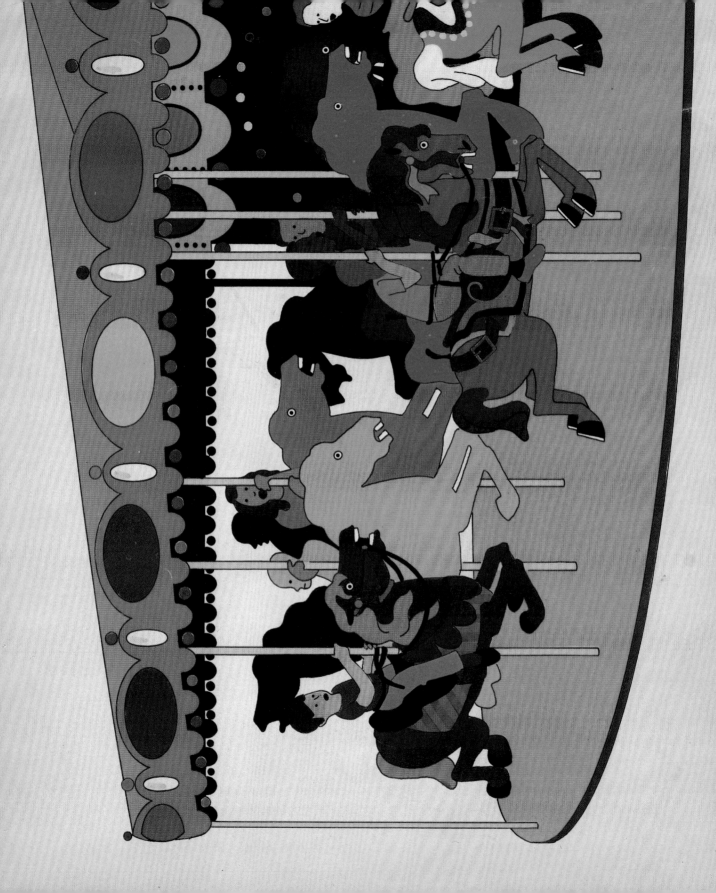

Stopping.

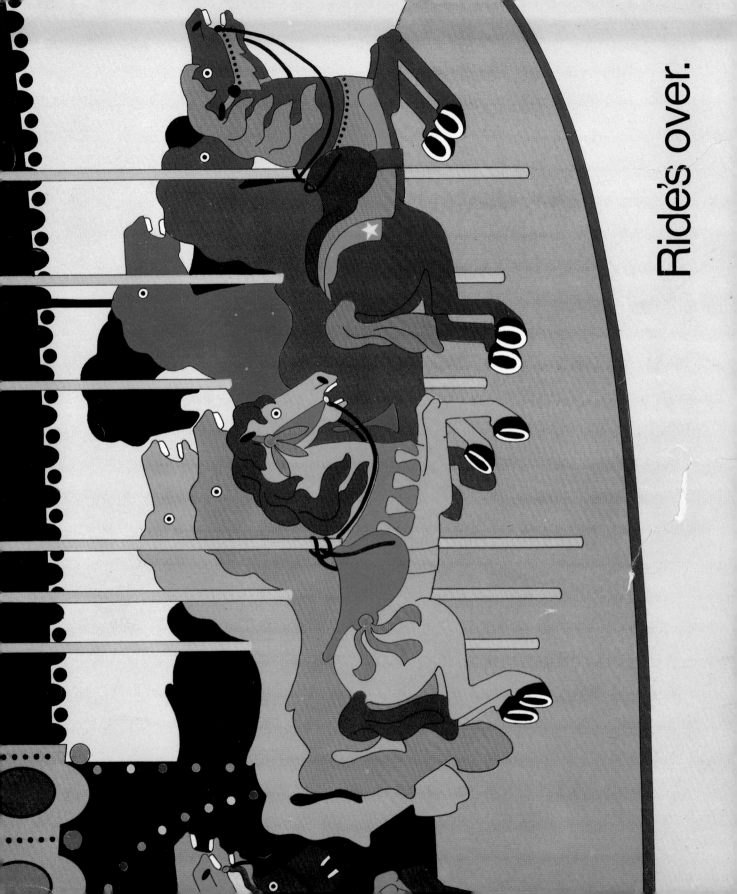

Ride's over.